TREVOR LAI

MY
BEST FRIEND
IS THE ONE
WHO BRINGS OUT
THE BEST IN ME
–HENRY FORD

BLOOMSBURY

NEW YORK   LONDON   OXFORD   NEW DELHI   SYDNEY

First published in the United States of America in December 2016
by Bloomsbury Children's Books
www.bloomsbury.com

Bloomsbury is a registered trademark of Bloomsbury Publishing Plc

For information about permission to reproduce selections from this book, write to
Permissions, Bloomsbury Children's Books, 1385 Broadway, New York, New York 10018
Bloomsbury books may be purchased for business or promotional use. For information on bulk purchases
please contact Macmillan Corporate and Premium Sales Department at specialmarkets@macmillan.com

Library of Congress Cataloging-in-Publication Data
Names: Lai, Trevor, author, illustrator.
Title: Piggy / by Trevor Lai.
Description: New York : Bloomsbury, 2016.
Summary: Piggy loved books so much he never had time for friends, but when he sees
a girl cat reading alone, he wonders if they could be best friends.
Identifiers: LCCN 2015046564 (print) | LCCN 2016022905 (e-book)
ISBN 978-1-68119-065-5 (hardcover)
ISBN 978-1-68119-066-2 (e-book) • ISBN 978-1-68119-067-9 (e-PDF)
Subjects: | CYAC: Books and reading—Fiction. | Friendship—Fiction. | BISAC: JUVENILE FICTION/
Social Issues/Friendship. | JUVENILE FICTION/Humorous Stories. | JUVENILE FICTION/Animals/Pigs.
Classification: LCC PZ7.1.L23 Pi 2016 (print) | LCC PZ7.1.L23 (e-book) | DDC [E]—dc23
LC record available at https://lccn.loc.gov/2015046564

Art created with pencil and watercolor and then finished digitally
Typeset in Jolly Good Proper
Book design by John Candell
Printed in China by Leo Paper Products, Heshan, Guangdong
2 4 6 8 10 9 7 5 3 1

All papers used by Bloomsbury Publishing, Inc., are natural, recyclable products
made from wood grown in well-managed forests. The manufacturing processes
conform to the environmental regulations of the country of origin.

To my family, for always believing in me.
Special thanks to Cat and Jen
for believing in Piggy.

There once was a little pig who loved to read. His name was Piggy, and he read day and night in his library.

His favorite stories were about friends who learned together and played together.

But Piggy was so busy reading, he did not have time to make friends.

One day, Piggy realized he was down to his last book. *I should save this happy ending*, he thought.

Piggy went into his storage room and picked the first toy he saw.

Soon, Piggy lost his kite but found something much better . . .

. . . a friend!

Well, the cat wasn't his friend *yet*.
She was busy reading her book.

So Piggy decided to get her attention.

Piggy went home to find something special.

He imagined how delighted his new
friend would be by his big, big bubbles.

Piggy ran left and right, and then he made a bubble that was *too* big!

The higher he floated, the more
he missed his cozy, safe library.

Piggy felt a bit down,
but when he looked
in the sky his spirits
were lifted again.

"I'll show her how high a pig can fly!"

Piggy soared into the air,
dipping and twirling his plane.

CAN WE BE FRIENDS?

He could not wait to see the cat's reaction . . .

. . . but she was not impressed!

When Piggy flew by,
she simply turned
the page.

Piggy had started pushing his plane back home when he noticed he was in a field of flowers.

"She'll love flowers! Lots of flowers!"

Piggy sent the cat all the flowers
the wind could carry.

But she didn't see them.
She just kept reading.

Piggy was sad that he didn't have a new friend.

At least I have my last book, Piggy thought.
I only wish I didn't have to read it alone.

And then he had an idea . . .

Piggy remembered that in his favorite stories, friends always shared with each other.

So he decided to share his last book with the cat.

She *was* excited to meet Piggy, after all. Her name was Kate.

But there was one problem: Kate couldn't see the words in Piggy's book clearly. Piggy knew exactly what his new friend needed.

Piggy brought Kate to his library and gave her special glasses.

And after the new friends finished reading together . . .

. . . they learned together and played together.

Kate was delighted by Piggy's big, big bubbles.

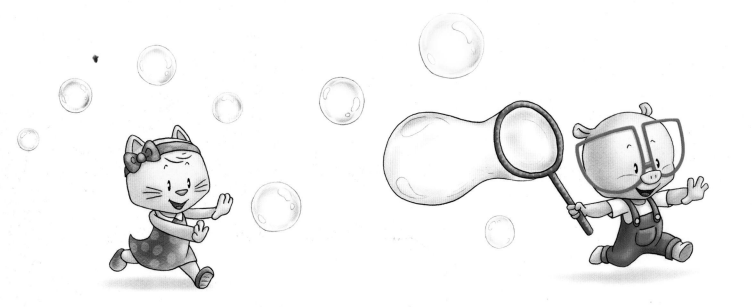

Piggy saw how high a cat could fly.

And every day was a happy ending.